No tickets . . .

Nancy was about to say that Bess should start working on a faster roller coaster design when she noticed Ned Nickerson, a boy in the fourth grade at the girls' school. He was running at full speed right toward them.

"Nancy! George! Bess!" Ned called out, breathless from running across the fairgrounds.

"Hi, Ned," Nancy greeted him. She liked Ned. He was a good friend. "What's up?"

"I'm so glad I found you," Ned said, trying to catch his breath. "My festival tickets . . . they're gone!"

NANCy DREW
AND THE CLUE CREW™

Ticket Trouble

By CAROLYN KEENE

ILLUSTRATED BY MACKY PAMINTUAN

SCHOLASTIC INC.

New York   Toronto   London   Auckland   Sydney
Mexico City   New Delhi   Hong Kong   Buenos Aires

ISBN-13: 978-0-545-11279-6
ISBN-10: 0-545-11279-6

12 11 10 9 8 7 6 5 4 3 2 1   8 9 10 11 12 13/0

Printed in the U.S.A.   40

First Scholastic printing, September 2008

Designed by Lisa Vega

The text of this book was set in ITC Stone Informal.

CONTENTS

ChAPTER ONE

Fall Festival

"Wow," eight-year-old Nancy Drew exclaimed. "This might be the best Fall Festival River Heights Elementary School has ever had!" Nancy walked under the multicolored balloon arch that divided the school parking lot from the athletic fields. Her best friends, George Fayne and Bess Marvin, followed her under the arch and over to the ticket booth.

"You'd never guess I played soccer on this field just yesterday," George commented, looking around her. "The decorating committee did a great job." She pointed past Nancy to some small stands covered with blinking bright lights. "Those arcade game booths are sitting where a soccer goal was in yesterday's game." George winked one brown eye, adding, "I know, because I scored three goals myself!"

Bess reached up and gave George a high five. She had to stand on her tiptoes, because George was a few inches taller than both her and Nancy. Even though Bess and George were first cousins, they didn't look very much alike. George had short brown hair and dark-chocolate-colored eyes. Bess had shoulder-length blond hair and blue eyes. Tonight Bess's hair was pulled back in a ponytail. George's was messy and sticking up a bit, like usual.

"It was your last goal that counted the most," Bess told her cousin. "When you stole the ball from Katherine Madison to score the winning point"—she cleared her throat—"I was screaming so loud, I nearly lost my voice. I thought Nancy was going to have a heart attack. She was jumping up and down and acting all crazy."

"Hey, look." Nancy interrupted their recap of George's big game. "There's an amusement ride area near the baseball diamond." From where they stood the girls could see a Tilt-A-Whirl, a bouncy house, and a roller coaster. "Let's go on the roller coaster first," Nancy suggested. "I bet we'll have a great view of the whole festival from the top of the first hill."

At the ticket booth the girls each bought a pack of twenty tickets. "My mom gave me enough money for a few rides, some arcade games, a hot dog, and a sweet treat," George told the others as she rolled her tickets up tightly and stuffed them into her front pocket.

"It's so great that the money goes back to the school, since this is a fund-raiser," Bess said, shoving her tickets into the small purse she was carrying.

Bess and George started walking toward the roller coaster when they noticed Nancy wasn't with them.

Nancy was still standing by the ticket booth, holding her tickets in her hand. Her blue eyes stared off into the distance. Her head was tilted, her left ear tipped way up. She was clearly listening to something.

"Nancy?" Bess waved her hands in front of her friend's face. "Anyone home?"

"Oh, sorry," Nancy said, coming back to earth. She pushed a loose strand of reddish-brown hair behind her ear. "I zoned out for a second."

Bess and George laughed. "We're used to that," George noted with a giggle. "You're super smart, fun to hang out with, and an amazing detective, but also easily—" George stopped, searching for the right word.

"Distracted," Bess supplied.

"Exactly," said George with a nod. "You're definitely easily distracted." She looked at Nancy, who was smiling, her head still tipped sideways. "What are you listening to?"

"A distraction," Nancy said, grinning. "Shh." She put her finger to her lips. "Do you hear it?"

"I hear carnival sounds," Bess put in. "I hear the whir of the rides, the plop of balls being thrown against metal milk jugs, and Principal

4

Newman announcing that she'll be revealing the winner of the chili cook-off in half an hour." She looked at George. "What do you hear?"

"I hear the new Best Buddies CD playing over the loudspeaker." George cupped her ear to listen better. "Ooh. I love this song." George shook her hips in time to the music and mouthed the words. "I asked my mom to get me this CD for Christmas."

"Listen closer," Nancy told her friends.

Silently the girls stood together, listening hard to hear whatever it was that Nancy heard.

"Augh," Bess suddenly cried. "It sounds like someone is singing along with the Best Buddies CD." She plugged her ears. "And whoever it is, they stink!" She turned to look at George.

"It's not me!" George insisted. "I was dancing, not singing!" She put her hands on her hips. "Besides, I'm not *that* bad a singer."

"Come on." Nancy stuck her own tickets in her pocket and grabbed her friends' hands. "There!" She pointed up to a carnival banner.

A large black bird was sitting on top of the banner, squawking along with the music. "Wow, that bird is really black. It must be a crow," Nancy remarked. "Crows are known to have loud, harsh chirps. This one is the worst."

The bird flew away and the girls, giggling, set off toward the first ride they wanted to go on. The bird followed them and landed in a tree near the Rockin' Racin' Roller Coaster. It settled 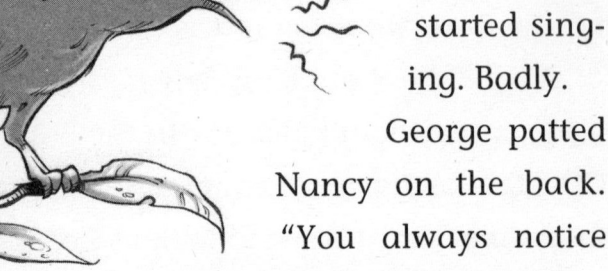 on a high branch and once again started singing. Badly.

George patted Nancy on the back. "You always notice things the rest of us miss."

"That's why Nancy has the detective notebook." Bess pointed to the small purple notebook poking out of Nancy's back pocket.

"It takes teamwork to figure out most mysteries." Nancy put her arms around her friends. "No matter where we are, if there is a mystery to be solved, the Clue Crew is on the case!"

"I bet there won't be any big mystery tonight." Bess took one last look at the bird with the screeching chirp and added, "Let's leave that crow to its singing. It's time to ride the roller coaster."

On their way to the ride, the girls saw Deirdre Shannon, Suzie Park, and Natalie Coleman standing near an ice-cream vendor, counting their tickets.

"Wow," Bess commented. "Those girls have a ton of tickets."

"Yeah," George said quietly. "I wonder why they need so many."

Nancy just shrugged. "Come on. Let's get on the roller coaster now. There's no line."

The girls ran to the gate and were able to hop right into a car on the ride. Mrs. Matterhorn, their third-grade math teacher, was taking tickets. "One ticket each, please," she told them. She tore their tickets in half, saying, "Nice to see you girls." Then to George, she added, "I ordered a new computer program for the math lab. If you have time after school Monday, I'd love to show it to you." Mrs. Matterhorn closed the car door and checked their seat belts.

George beamed. She was good at math, but there was nothing she liked more than computers. "I'll be there," she called out as the roller coaster carried them high into the air.

"Check this out," said Nancy as they reached the top of the coaster. "You really can see everything from here." Nancy pointed out Deirdre, Suzie, and Natalie playing over in the arcade gaming area.

Bess saw Hannah Gruen, Nancy's housekeeper, leaning over a pot on the chili cook-off stage.

"I can't wait to taste her chili," said George. "Hannah's a great cook."

"Hannah has been trying new chili recipes at dinner every night for the past two weeks," Nancy said, rubbing her belly. "Last night I was begging for a pizza." The girls all laughed. They came down the first hill with a zoom and screamed until the end of the ride.

"That was great," Bess declared when they exited the ride. "But if I could invent my own type of roller coaster, it would be bigger, go higher, and flip around more. Maybe the cars could even go sideways. . . . " Bess's voice tapered off as she began imagining the possibilities. She loved inventing things.

Nancy was about to say that Bess should start working on a faster roller coaster design when she noticed Ned Nickerson, a boy in the fourth grade at the girls' school. He was running at full speed right toward them.

"Nancy! George! Bess!" Ned called out, breathless from running across the fairgrounds.

"Hi, Ned," Nancy greeted him. She liked Ned. He was a good friend. "What's up?"

"I'm so glad I found you," Ned said, trying to catch his breath. "My festival tickets . . . they're gone!"

CHAPTER TWO

Ticket Trouble

"I need your help! You have to solve a mystery," Ned said. He grabbed Nancy by the hand and started pulling her toward the Perfect Pitch baseball-throwing booth. Bess and George fell in beside them. They had to jog to keep up.

"I was standing right here when my tickets disappeared." Ned showed the girls where he'd set his tickets down on the wooden countertop while he took his turn. He had three tries to knock over a pyramid made out of metal milk jugs.

"I only knocked down one of the three jugs," Ned explained. "Then I reached over to get one more ticket to try again. That's when I noticed my tickets were missing." He put his head in his hands. "Aww, man," he said sadly. "I raked leaves all week to get extra money for the festival. My mom got me a few tickets. Then I bought twenty more with my own hard-earned cash." He shook his mop of brown hair. "My mom will be so disappointed if I tell her I lost the tickets. She told me to keep them safely in my pocket. I didn't listen. There's no way she's going to buy me more."

Ned told Nancy that he wrote his initials, *NN*, on the back of each ticket. "I've only used one ticket so far. Just here at this booth. I wanted to win one of those stuffed teddy bears." He pointed at the big prizes behind the counter.

"Did you check your pockets?" asked George.

"Maybe you put the tickets away and forgot about them."

"I've checked everywhere," Ned replied, turning his jeans pockets inside out. "Empty." He looked at the ground. "I also searched under the baseball booth counter and at the dart game next door." He let out a big sigh. "They're simply gone."

"Amazing as it seems, it looks like I was wrong," Bess declared. "There *is* a mystery to be solved tonight."

Nancy pinched her lips together thoughtfully. Then she pulled out her purple notebook. At the top of a clean white page, she wrote down *Ned's Missing Festival Tickets*. Then she, Bess, and George began to look around for clues.

Even though Ned said he checked under the countertop, Nancy decided to look there again. She didn't think she'd find his tickets, but maybe there was a clue hidden on the ground. She got down on her hands and knees and searched around in the dirt.

Bess and George asked Ned to tell his story again from the beginning and, this time, to act out his every move.

Ned stood behind the yellow line on the ground and leaned over the counter, pretending he was throwing a baseball.

Bess asked him to show her where he put his feet. She wanted to know precisely what angle he threw at.

"You see," Bess told Ned, "arcade games are fun, but they're rigged so that it's really hard to win." Because Bess understood how the games worked, she explained, "There is usually lead or something heavy in the bottom of the milk jugs, making them hard to tip over. They might tip back a bit when you get them with a fast ball, but more often than not, they'll just pop right back up again."

"That's what happened to me!" Ned exclaimed. "I thought I hit them really hard, but only the top one fell over."

"You're such a good ballplayer, I'm sure

you threw a hard one. It's just that the game is designed so that people will have to spend a lot of tickets to score a prize." Bess squinted at the jugs.

She opened her purse, took out one of her tickets, and put it on the counter. One of the third-grade parents, Mr. Evans, was taking tickets. He tore Bess's ticket in half and set out three balls.

"The trick is to slam the ball directly between two of the jugs on the bottom row," Bess explained as she picked up one ball. "The whole pyramid will come down if you can knock those two over." Then, just to prove her point, Bess tossed the ball, not hard but with perfect aim. She hit the bottom jugs just as she'd said, and all three milk jugs toppled.

Bess grinned and shrugged while she gathered the large stuffed bear prize in her arms.

"Good job." Ned beamed. But his smile turned into a frown when he added, "I'd love to use your technique. If only I had my tickets,

I'm sure I could win a bear if I tried now."

"Don't worry, Ned," said Bess, trying to cheer him up. "We'll find them."

"Can you show us exactly where you put your tickets while you were playing?" George asked.

"I set them right next to me like this." Reaching out, Ned acted like he was putting tickets on the counter. "Then I played the game." He rounded up his pitching arm as if he was about to make a throw but stopped suddenly as a black crow swooped past.

"Hey!" Ned called after the bird, which had nearly bumped into his arm.

"That bird is a bad singer *and* a reckless

flyer," Nancy remarked with a laugh.

George inspected the countertop. It was made out of wood and painted bright red. "Hey, Nancy, check this out," she called after a few seconds of investigating. "I think I found our first clue."

Nancy peered at the countertop. She saw a long, deep scratch where the red paint had been peeled off. The scratch was in exactly the same place where Ned said he'd set down his tickets. Nancy thought for a moment. Then she turned to Mr. Evans.

"When was this counter painted?" she asked him.

"Yesterday," reported Mr. Evans. "We wanted everything to look fresh and new for the festival tonight."

"Very interesting," Nancy said, bending down close to get a better look at the scratch. "George," she said at last, "you're right. This *is* a clue. This scratch must be new. It looks like it was made by something pointy. Something that dug into the countertop." Nancy pulled out her notebook and wrote down: *Red paint scratch mark*. Then she closed the notebook's purple cover and put it back in her pocket.

"Maybe if someone stole the tickets, they scratched the counter with their fingernail as they grabbed them," George suggested.

"We could look at everyone's nails," Bess put in. "Whoever has red paint under their nails must have taken Ned's tickets."

Nancy glanced around. The festival was really crowded. Looking at everyone's fingernails would take way too long. They needed more clues.

"So did you figure it out yet?" asked Ned impatiently.

"We only have one clue," Nancy reported. "And so far, no suspects. We need a little more time."

George reached into her pocket. "Here," she said, carefully tearing a single ticket off her own stack. "You can borrow one of my tickets. Go buy a soda and hang out for a while. We'll come get you when we know something."

Ned took the ticket. "Thanks," he said. "I really want my tickets back before the festival is over."

"No problem," Nancy told Ned. "We'll find your tickets."

"No mystery is too difficult," Bess agreed.

George smiled, adding, "The Clue Crew is on the case."

ChaPTER ThREE

Suspicious Suspects

As soon as Ned walked off, Bess turned to Nancy and asked, "What do we do next? I didn't want to admit it to Ned, but it kinda seems like we're at a dead end. We have only one clue, no witnesses, and no suspects."

Nancy looked around and bit her bottom lip. "We promised Ned we'd solve the mystery, so I guess we should get busy searching for more clues."

"Yeah. But where should we look?" Bess said with a shrug. "We already covered the baseball arcade."

"I have an idea about where to start," said George suddenly. "Check out Deirdre, Suzie, and Natalie." She pointed at the girls, who were standing nearby under a tree. The bad-singing crow was sitting high on a branch above them. Deirdre, Suzie, and Natalie were counting their tickets.

"Those girls had a lot of tickets when we first got to the Fall Festival," George remarked. "It

looks like they have even more now."

"When we were on the roller coaster, we saw them over by the baseball booth," said Bess. "If they were spending their tickets, they'd have a smaller stack, not a bigger one." She clicked her tongue. "Unless maybe they took Ned's tickets."

Nancy opened her purple notebook and began to write down Deirdre, Suzie, and Natalie as possible suspects. "Hang on a second." She put away her pencil and closed the notebook with a snap. "We can't accuse those girls of stealing Ned's tickets without any real proof. I think we'd better go talk to them."

"That's a good plan." Bess hugged her new stuffed bear to her chest. "If they didn't take Ned's tickets, maybe they saw or heard something that would help us."

"Come on," George said, leading the way across the grass.

Nancy, Bess, and George had taken only a few steps when Ned came rushing up. "Did ya find my tickets?" he cried excitedly. "Did ya?"

"Did ya finish your soda already?" Nancy asked, imitating the way he was speaking.

Ned laughed. "Yeah," he admitted. "I drank the whole thing in one gulp."

"Well," George said, taking her time and speaking very slowly, "we have a plan, but we haven't solved the mystery yet."

"There's only one more hour of the festival." Ned sighed. "I really want to win a stuffed bear. Time's running out. I gotta get my tickets back."

"We're working on it." Bess smiled and reached into her purse. She pulled out one ticket and handed it to Ned. "You can have one of my tickets. Go get an ice cream, okay? We'll come find you soon."

"You guys are nice to keep giving me tickets," said Ned. "I'll pay you back as soon as I have my own tickets again." He thanked Bess and hurried away.

"Do you think we can solve this mystery in less than an hour?" George asked Nancy.

"Sure," Nancy stated confidently. She headed

out toward the tree where Deirdre had been hanging with her friends. "Hmm," she said before they got there. "I still think we can solve the mystery, but we have a little problem."

"What's wrong?" asked George, but she didn't need Nancy to tell her what was up. Deirdre, Suzie, and Natalie were gone. During the few minutes Nancy and her friends had been talking to Ned, the other girls had disappeared back into the crowded festival.

Bess scanned the crowd with her eyes squinted. "There," she cheered after she'd taken a good hard look around the fair. "I see Deirdre over by the apple bobbing."

"And I spy Suzie at the chili cook-off," George added.

Nancy searched all around for Natalie but didn't find her. "They split up," she remarked. "Let's go talk to Deirdre first."

"We have another problem," Bess told the other girls. "I don't think we should rush off to interview Deirdre quite yet."

"Why not?" George and Nancy said at the same time.

"Well," Bess went on, clearly trying to hide a smile, "you know how easily distracted Nancy can be. She might trip and fall on our way." She pointed down at Nancy's untied shoelace.

Nancy giggled. "Thanks, Bess. I'm glad you are here to protect me," she said, bending down to tie her shoe. She stayed bent over for a full minute before George suggested, "We should get going before Deirdre disappears in the crowd again."

Nancy didn't stand up or even answer. She stayed hunched over in shoe-tying position, staring at something by the tree trunk.

"Earth to Nancy!" Bess called. "Are you stuck down there?"

"Oh," Nancy said, standing up suddenly. "I zoned out again. Sorry. This time I was tying my shoe when something under the tree caught my eye. I was trying to figure out what it was." She moved closer to the tree trunk.

Under the tree, Nancy reached down and

picked up a small piece of yellow paper. "The yellow color stood out in the festival lights," she told her friends. "I knew it wasn't a leaf, but couldn't guess what it might be."

"It looks like a ripped and dirty piece of trash to me," said George. "We should throw it out to help keep the school clean."

"No. . . . It's a torn half of a ticket," Nancy murmured.

"Definitely trash." George looked over Nancy's shoulder. "Every ticket-taker at the festival is ripping tickets in half. This one probably fell out of someone's garbage bag."

Nancy was holding up the little paper, examining it.

"Hang on a second. That's not trash!" Bess exclaimed. She was standing in front of Nancy. While Nancy was looking at one side of the ticket, Bess could clearly see the other side. "There is writing on the back of that ticket. I see an *N* on it!" Bess was so excited, she was shouting. "Nancy just found our second clue!"

Nancy flipped the ticket over in her hand. Bess was right. The ticket was definitely a clue. There was a capital *N* written in black ink on the back of the torn yellow ticket.

Ned said that he had written *NN* on the back of his tickets. There was no doubt about it: This was one of Ned's missing tickets.

Nancy pulled out her notebook and wrote *Torn ticket* under the words *Red paint scratch mark*. Now they had two clues. And because they found Ned's ticket right where Deirdre, Suzie, and Natalie had been standing only minutes before, they also had the proof they needed.

Deirdre, Suzie, and Natalie were officially suspects in the Mystery of Ned's Missing Festival Tickets.

ChAPTER FOUR

Apple Attack

The girls hustled through the crowd toward the Apple Attack apple-bobbing booth. On the way they saw their gym teacher, who was dressed as a juggler. He was standing high on stilts, easily tossing five multicolored balls between his hands.

"What's your hurry?" Mr. Wilson called down to Bess. "Where's the fire?"

"No fire," Bess called back.

"I see," said Mr. Wilson. "Well then, knowing you girls, there must be a mystery to solve."

"How'd you guess?" George asked. She was still walking very fast and talking as she passed by.

"Check out Nancy Drew," Mr. Wilson replied

with a chuckle. Bess and George turned around to look at Nancy. Sure she was walking fast, like they were, but she was also double-checking the clues in her purple notebook as she went along. "It doesn't take a detective to know that the Clue Crew is trying to solve a mystery," Mr. Wilson explained. "But you should tell her that if she's going to investigate and walk at the same time, she'd better tie her shoelace."

"Thanks, Mr. Wilson," George said. "We'll tell her."

Bess and George waited for Nancy to catch up. "Nancy," Bess told her friend, "you still forgot to tie your shoe."

Nancy looked up at Bess and shook her head. "Oh, yeah," she said, putting the notebook back into her jeans pocket. "I guess I got distracted when I found part of Ned's ticket in the dirt." Nancy bent down and finally tied her shoe. This time she stood right back up. There weren't any other clues in the grass by her feet.

Nancy smiled up at Mr. Wilson and waved.

"Before you girls hurry off," Mr. Wilson said, "can one of you toss up that soccer ball over there?" He pointed to a bag of balls of all shapes and sizes sitting near a trash can. "I want to juggle these five little balls, plus a soccer ball, too."

"You're the soccer star, George," said Bess as she got the ball out of the bag. "You should toss it up to him."

"Careful now," Mr. Wilson warned. "You have to throw it when my left hand is empty." The girls watched the five balls popping up and down, back and forth between his hands. "Ready?" he asked.

"Ready." George pulled back the ball.

"Aim," said Mr. Wilson.

George squinted her eyes, staring at Mr. Wilson's left hand.

"Fire!" he called, and George released the ball with a snap.

It sailed through the air and landed perfectly in Mr. Wilson's left hand. He easily added the

soccer ball to his juggling routine
without falling off his stilts.

The girls began to clap and
cheer.

Mr. Wilson took a
little bow. A very little
bow, since he didn't
want to lose
his focus.

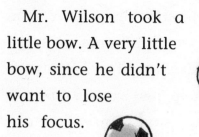

"Want to tell me about the mystery?" he asked before the girls walked on.

"Ned's carnival tickets are missing," Bess told their teacher.

"I'm sure you girls will find them," Mr. Wilson said as the soccer ball went sailing through the air. He caught it and tossed it right back up again. "But if you need any help, just let me know."

"Thanks, Mr. Wilson," said Nancy. She took one last look down at her shoe to make sure it was still tied before rushing off with Bess and George to find Deirdre.

Deirdre was waiting her turn for apple bobbing. The girls lined up behind her.

When Deirdre saw Nancy, Bess, and George, she said, "If you get an apple in your mouth, not only do you get to keep the apple, but you get a stuffed bear, too." She showed them the bears hanging from a portable wall. They were exactly the same kind of bears that were at the baseball arcade, the same kind that Bess had already won.

"I really want a bear," Deirdre told them. "I simply *have* to win one."

"Hmm," whispered George, leaning into Nancy and Bess. "Maybe Deirdre took Ned's tickets so she'd have more chances to win." George watched a boy from their class trying his luck. After using three tickets, the mom running the booth told him he had to go to the back of the line if he wanted to try again.

It was Deirdre's turn next. They would wait to ask about her tickets until after she went bobbing.

"The trick to apple bobbing is using math," George explained as Deirdre put on the yellow plastic poncho and tied back her hair with a pink ribbon. "The apples move in an arc through the water. I wish I had my computer, because I could diagram an apple's trajectory. It's really interesting."

"I'm sure it is," said Bess, yawning big. "Interesting to you."

"Hey," George countered. "We listened to you talk about how the baseball arcade works. It's my turn."

Bess giggled. "I'm kidding, George. I think it's cool to know how math works in the real world." She watched as Deirdre came up out of the water, dripping wet, with her mouth empty. Deirdre tore off a second ticket from her large wad, handed it to the mom, and dunked her head in again. "

George beamed. She was smiling so big that her eyes crinkled up. "Using math, I bet I could win the apple bobbing on the first try." She pulled out her tickets and tore one off. "Using basic physics, the size and weight of the apple make it bob in the water. The bigger the apple, the harder it is to grab with your teeth. You have to go for a small one."

Deirdre came up for air and handed the booth mom a third ticket for her final try. Water was dripping off her chin and nose. She looked frustrated.

When Deirdre put her head back into the bucket, George said, "You've gotta grab a small one fast before it moves away or push it to the bottom of the barrel and pin it with your teeth."

The girls watched Deirdre lift her face out of the bucket. She hadn't been able to snag an apple. She took off the poncho and handed it to George, saying, "If you think it's so easy, let's see you do it." As Deirdre untied her hair, that crazy crow swooshed in and snagged the pink hair ribbon right out of her hand.

"That's one nutty bird," Deirdre remarked.

"Good thing I have new hair ribbons at home."

George slipped the plastic poncho over her head, ready to bob, and handed the booth mom a ticket.

It happened so fast. George dunked her head into the apple-bobbing barrel and not even a second later came up with an apple firmly clenched in her teeth. She spit the apple into her hand. "I went for a small one and followed it on its arc through the water." George winked. "Easy as apple pie."

The booth mom handed George her stuffed teddy bear prize.

Deirdre put her hands on her hips and huffed. "I definitely need more tickets if I'm going to win a bear."

"Speaking of tickets," Nancy said, "we were wondering where you got so many."

"My dad gave them to me," Deirdre replied. "He promised I could have as many tickets as I needed if I helped him clean out the garage. It was *soooo* gross and took up an entire Sunday, but it was totally worth it!" And with that, Deirdre stomped away to find her dad.

"Deirdre didn't take the tickets," Bess said thoughtfully. "If she can get more by asking her dad for them, she wouldn't need to steal Ned's."

Nancy pulled out her purple notebook and pencil. She opened to Ned's ticket mystery page and crossed Deirdre off her list of suspects.

"We're right by the chili cook-off stage. That's where we saw Suzie." George pointed across the grass to a crowded area.

"And just like Deirdre, Suzie sure had a lot of tickets in her hand," added Bess.

Nancy studied her notes and then closed the notebook cover. "Suzie and Natalie are still suspects. Let's go find Suzie next."

CHAPTER FIVE

Chili Challenge

The girls were running over to the chili cook-off stage when George suddenly stopped and put a hand around her ear. "Do you hear that?" she said.

"Is it that pesky crow again?" Nancy asked, tilting her head to listen. "It disappeared after taking Deirdre's ribbon. I don't see it now. I don't hear it either."

"It's not the crow," George said. "Listen carefully."

"Do you mean the Best Buddies CD?" Bess asked. "They're playing your favorite song from it right now."

"No," George said with a smile. "It's Principal

Newman announcing that the chili awards will be given out in ten minutes."

The girls moved a little faster, hustling past the cotton candy vendor and the popcorn booth. "Yum," Bess said. The smell of popcorn followed them through the crowd. "We'd better solve this mystery fast. I need a snack."

"Good thing we're headed to the chili cook-off," Nancy replied. "There are ten different types and you can taste them all." She paused and then added, "After we talk to Suzie, of course."

"There she is." George spotted Suzie's light pink jacket in the crowd. She was standing next to a large black chili pot.

"She's about to taste my mom's chili," George said proudly. George's mom, Mrs. Fayne, was a caterer in River Heights. "Everyone loves Mom's chili."

"Your mom might have won last year," said Nancy, "but Hannah is determined to take first place this time."

Just then, a familiar voice called out, "Girls!"

Nancy recognized the voice immediately. It was Hannah.

"Come over and taste my chili first." Hannah waved at them. "There are only a few minutes left before the judge hands out the prize ribbons."

Nancy looked over at Suzie. Mrs. Fayne was handing her a little bowl of chili and a plastic spoon.

"We don't want to be rude to Hannah," George said to her friends. "Let's stop and taste her chili, but we'd better make it fast." George smiled at Bess. "Besides, Bess is hungry. Investigating mysteries is hard work. We should get her a chili snack."

Bess grinned and walked straight over to Hannah's bright red chili pot. "Hello, Ms. Gruen," she said politely.

Hannah was wearing an apron that read "Kiss the Cook." So Nancy did what it said. She gave Hannah a little hello kiss on the cheek.

Hannah handed each of the girls a miniature

bowl with a bit of chili and a plastic spoon. "If you like it," she said, "you can come over tomorrow. We'll be having leftovers for lunch."

Nancy took her taster bowl but rolled her eyes. "No offense, but I don't think I can stomach any more chili, Hannah." She closed her eyes, remembering the many different ways Hannah had served her test batches of chili.

"Over the past two weeks, we've had chili dogs, chili fries, chili nachos, chili pot pie, and even frozen chili popsicles." Nancy stuck out her tongue. "That was the grossest thing ever."

Bess tasted Hannah's chili sample and said, "Nancy's just spoiled, having a good cook like you living with her." She licked her lips. "This chili is amazing. I'll be at your place for lunch for sure!" Bess gobbled up the little bowl and even asked Hannah for a second sample.

"What do you think, George?" Hannah asked after George had taken a taste.

"If I say it's better than my mom's, I'll be in big trouble." George smiled. "But it is really, really good."

Everyone turned to Nancy, who hadn't tasted the chili yet.

Nancy was holding the spoon near her mouth, but her lips wouldn't open. "I just can't eat more chili," she told Hannah. "I want to. But after days and days of it, I am full to the top."

"You won't even taste it for the contest?"

asked Hannah. "I changed the recipe since you had it last. I added a secret ingredient." Hannah appealed to Nancy's detective side. "I bet you can't figure out what the secret is," she challenged.

Nancy let out a big breath and groaned, "You know I can't resist a mystery." She took a bite of the chili, then remarked, "Wow! This is your best pot yet." She closed her eyes, letting the taste of the chili roll around on her tongue. "Not pepper. Not cinnamon." Nancy wrinkled her nose. "I've got it. This mystery is solved." She opened her eyes.

"So what's the ingredient?" asked George.

"Do you really know?" Bess wondered aloud.

Nancy looked to Hannah. It was her secret recipe, after all. Nancy wasn't sure if she should tell everyone or not.

"After the contest," Hannah told her, "the school is printing a booklet of all the recipes. The secret won't be a secret after that. Go ahead, Detective Nancy Drew, tell us what you think the mystery ingredient is."

Nancy took another bite just to be certain, then said, "Chocolate. Hannah melted chocolate into her chili."

Hannah started to laugh. "You are a great detective, Nancy." She ruffled Nancy's hair. "I'm proud of you."

"What a great idea," George said. "I know my mom didn't do anything cool like that to her chili. My mom's chili is good, but yours is really special. I bet you'll win after all." George winked at Hannah. "Save me a bowl. I'm coming for lunch tomorrow, too. Just don't tell my mom!" she added with a laugh.

Bess put her arm around Nancy. "Now that the chili mystery is solved, we'd better help Ned with his ticket mystery."

The girls said good-bye to Hannah and wished her good luck, then hurried over to Mrs. Fayne's chili pot. Luckily, Suzie was still there.

"Hello, girls," Mrs. Fayne greeted them. "Did you come to taste my chili?"

"Do we have to?" Nancy whispered to George. "I know it's the polite thing to do, but I just can't eat another bite. Honestly."

"No problem," George told Nancy. Turning to her mom, she said, "Actually, we just came to talk to Suzie."

"All right." Mrs. Fayne wasn't upset. "I know you girls ate my chili last year. Since I won first place, I didn't change the recipe at all."

"Watch out for Hannah Gruen," George warned her mom. "She has a killer recipe this year."

"It would be lovely if I won again, but I won't be upset if Hannah takes first place this time. I hear she added a secret ingredient," Mrs. Fayne remarked, picking up a wooden spoon and stirring her pot. "I wonder what it is."

Nancy winked. "It's a mystery. But the secret will be revealed in a few days in the school recipe booklet."

"I suppose I'll have to wait patiently until then." Mrs. Fayne turned away from the girls to serve Police Chief McGinnis a taste of her chili.

Suzie threw away her empty bowl and said to Nancy, Bess, and George, "You wanted to talk to me?"

"We noticed that you have a lot of festival tickets," Bess told Suzie.

"I need a lot of tickets because I *have* to win a bear," Suzie explained.

"We were wondering where you got so many—," Nancy began, but her voice was drowned out by Principal Newman talking over the loudspeaker. She was announcing the winner of the chili cook-off. "After much tasting and testing, the winner of this year's chili cook-off is . . . "

ChaPTER Six

Dart Dare

". . . Hannah Gruen!"

"Hannah gets the blue ribbon!" George exclaimed. "That's great news."

"Do you think your mom will be bummed?" asked Nancy. She was excited for Hannah and honestly concerned about Mrs. Fayne's feelings at the same time.

"Not a chance," George reassured her. "Mom even said she thought Hannah should win this year."

Bess added, "After all the experimenting Hannah did, she probably worked the hardest to win. She totally deserves first place."

"I'm glad she won," Nancy remarked, holding

her belly. "Hopefully next year she'll enter the pie bake-off instead." She laughed. "I'd love to spend two weeks tasting pie samples. With yummy ice cream."

Suzie turned to George. "I want to be a caterer like your mom when I grow up, so I was hanging out at the cook-off, trying to learn a little about cooking chili. Now I'd better get back to trying to win a stuffed bear." She checked her watch. "I'm running out of time. If you want to talk, come with me to the arcade area."

The girls followed Suzie over to the Dart Dare throwing game. Nancy noticed the noisy crow sitting on top of the Dart Dare sign.

"Hi, girls," Nancy's dad said. Mr. Drew was taking tickets and handing out the darts at the booth. "Are you having a good time?"

"We're on a case, Dad," Nancy told him.

"I want to hear about it after the festival," Mr. Drew said. "This line is growing pretty long, so right now I need to focus on the dart game."

"Sure, Dad. Hopefully, we'll solve this mystery

soon. I'll fill you in during the car ride home,"
Nancy told her father. "We need to speak to
Suzie now, anyway."

By now Suzie was at the front of the line. "We
can talk after I play," she said, tearing off one
ticket from the huge stack in her hand and giving it to Mr. Drew. Nancy watched as her father
ripped Suzie's ticket in half and gave her three
darts. He told her Suzie needed to throw them
hard at the colored balloons at the back of the
booth. "You only have to pop one balloon to
win a bear," Mr. Drew explained.

Suzie picked up a dart. Before she threw it, she
looked at George and Bess. "Any ideas on how I
can win this game?" she asked them.

"Even if you threw on a precise curve," George
said after carefully thinking about how the
game was played, "there is the rebound off the
balloon." She shook her head. "Math won't help
you win this one."

Bess bit her bottom lip before answering. "Like
the baseball game, this is designed so that you

will probably lose and have to spend more tickets. The darts are dull and the balloons are placed close together to make it hard to hit just one. Chances are good the dart will fall between the balloons." Bess shrugged. "I think it's best to just cross your fingers for luck, then throw the dart."

Suzie decided that instead of crossing her fingers, she would hold her lucky necklace. "Will you hold my tickets for me?" she asked Nancy. "I need one hand to throw the dart and the other to squeeze my lucky necklace."

Nancy was glad to help. She took Suzie's stack of tickets from her, glancing at them

before closing her fist around the plain yellow tickets. "I'll keep your tickets safe," she told Suzie.

"Thanks," Suzie said. Then she tossed the first dart. It bounced off a red balloon and fell to the ground. Mr. Drew picked it up and put it in his apron pocket. Suzie tossed the second dart. It hit a blue balloon, but instead of popping, the balloon spun a little and the dart dropped away.

Suzie rubbed her necklace. She closed her eyes and said, "I wish I would pop a balloon." Pulling her hand back for the throw, Suzie squinted one eye and took careful aim. She released the dart. It sailed through the air, headed directly for a yellow balloon.

Pop.

"I did it!" she shouted. "I can't believe it!" Suzie pointed up at the stuffed bears on a shelf behind Mr. Drew. "Good thing I was wearing my lucky necklace." Mr. Drew handed Suzie a teddy bear. She was so happy that she kept hugging the bear and jumping around.

"Girls," Mr. Drew called out to the friends from behind the dart booth. "Will you do me a favor?"

Bess and George really wanted to interview Suzie right away, but Nancy got a faraway look in her eye as she told them they were no longer in a hurry. She wanted to help her dad before they did anything else. Nancy moved closer to the booth counter, saying, "What's up?"

"I need you to cut off a few pieces of string for me while I inflate a new yellow balloon." Mr. Drew handed Nancy a ball of brown twine and a pair of scissors. He showed her how long to make the pieces. "I need to tie up the new balloon for the next person who wants to play the game."

Mr. Drew scratched his head. "The funny thing is that I swear I cut up a whole bunch of string pieces just before Suzie took her turn." He looked down at the bright blue countertop. "I thought I put them here on the counter."

Then he looked inside his
apron pocket, pulling out some
torn tickets and a handful of flat balloons.
Mr. Drew shook his head. "I've been so busy I
probably thought I cut up the string, but didn't
actually do it."

Bess and George helped Nancy as she cut a piece of string for her dad. Mr. Drew blew up a balloon, took the string, and tied the balloon to the board. Then Nancy cut a few extra pieces for him.

Mr. Drew took the pieces and put them in his apron pocket. "Thanks, Pudding Pie. Now I'll be able to put up balloons when I need to." He tapped the front of the pocket before going back to work taking tickets, ripping them in half, and handing out darts.

"We still need to talk to Suzie," Bess said, getting back to business. "But where'd she go?" Bess realized that while Nancy had been cutting string, Suzie had wandered away.

Just then, Ned came rushing up to the dart booth. "Did you find my tickets?" he asked Nancy and the Clue Crew.

Nancy was sorry to have to tell Ned that they hadn't found his tickets yet. She opened her notebook and took out her pencil. "We still have one more suspect to interview."

"I thought we had two suspects," Bess said, leaning in and correcting Nancy. "We were about to interview Suzie."

"No, I'm sure that now we only have one suspect left," Nancy replied. "Suzie didn't take Ned's tickets." She drew a line through Suzie's name.

"What?!" Bess and George said at the same time.

Nancy closed her notebook and explained, "When I was holding Suzie's tickets, I checked them out. All her tickets were plain yellow. There wasn't any writing on the back."

"Suzie wanted to win a stuffed bear so badly, I thought she nabbed Ned's tickets so she could get extra chances. I was sure we'd solved this mystery, but I was wrong," said George. "I guess we'd better go find Natalie. She's our last suspect."

"What if Natalie didn't take my tickets?" Ned asked. "What will the Clue Crew do then?"

"We'll start looking for more clues," Nancy

told him. "Don't worry, Ned. We won't let you down."

"I totally believe that you will solve this mystery." Ned looked around the carnival. It was getting late and people were already starting to head home for the evening. "But can you hurry up? The festival is almost over."

ChaPTeR SeVeN

Tall Teacher

"Here, Ned," Nancy said, carefully ripping off one of her own tickets. "Do you want to get some popcorn? You could eat it while we interview Natalie."

"I think I should come with you," Ned suggested. "Just in case she really did take them." He looked at Nancy seriously. "I've seen situations exactly like this one on TV. The thieves always try to run away. I could be your backup."

Nancy smiled. "Thanks for the offer, but we aren't going to accuse Natalie of stealing. The Clue Crew interviews suspects and looks for clues. We never just march up and blame someone. She might be our last suspect, but right now all we're going to do is ask her a few questions."

"Then we process the information and discuss the possibilities," George added. "That's why solving mysteries isn't a quick business."

"Hopefully Natalie will provide the information we need to solve this mystery," Bess said, still hugging the bear she'd won at the baseball booth.

"Wow," Ned exclaimed. "I didn't realize that detective work took so much thinking. It seems kind of hard the way you explain it."

"It's not hard when you know what you're doing," Nancy said with a grin.

"Well, then." Ned took the yellow ticket from Nancy. "I'll leave Natalie's interview to the professionals. I'm not hungry, so I'm going to take this ticket over to the arcade and throw three baseballs at milk jugs instead."

"Good luck," said Nancy. Then, before Ned walked away, she added, "I'll let you know if—I mean, when—we solve the mystery."

"Great," Ned replied. Then, after a short pause, he continued, "This is the last ticket I'm borrowing." He held up the ticket Nancy had given him. "If you don't find my tickets soon, I'm going home."

Ned was still having a pretty good time, but Nancy could tell that if they didn't find his tickets soon, he was going to go home feeling sad that he'd missed a lot of the festival fun.

"We'd better hurry and talk to Natalie," Nancy said, and then told Ned that they would move as fast as they could.

"Don't forget," Ned called after them as the girls strode off, "if you need backup, I'll be at the baseball-throwing booth using Bess's tips and Nancy's ticket to try to win a bear." He laughed. "You might be good at solving mysteries, but I'm a superfast runner! And a good defensive tackle."

The girls were still giggling at the idea that the Clue Crew might need "backup" when they realized they were wandering around the festival aimlessly. They actually had no idea where to find Natalie, and in the confusion of Ned rushing up to them at the Dart Dare booth, they'd lost track of Suzie as well.

"So much for hurrying to solve this mystery," Bess moaned. "We can't even find our number one suspect!"

"I wonder if Suzie was going to meet up with her," George remarked. "I bet if we'd followed

Suzie she'd have led us straight to Natalie."

"We're going to have to search out Natalie a different way," Nancy said, standing on her tiptoes and peering through the crowd. "I wish I could see farther. . . . " Suddenly Nancy's voice dropped and she got that far-off look in her eyes.

"Don't zone out again." George gave Nancy's shoulder a little shake. "We promised Ned we'd move quickly."

"I wasn't zoning." Nancy blinked twice to clear her head. "Well, maybe just a little." She smiled. "I was thinking about how we could see a bigger area of the festival."

"We could get back on the roller coaster," Bess suggested. "We could see everything from the top."

"We don't have time to wait in line," said Nancy, pointing at the big crowd of kids now waiting for the ride.

"Or we could ask that annoying crow for a lift." George pointed at the crow, who was now perched on the back of a nearby bench.

Nancy noticed that the crow had something in its mouth. She inched closer to get a better look and saw a bit of white fluff hanging from the bird's beak. *Interesting,* she thought. "I bet the crow has a bird's-eye view from way up there!" George began to laugh at her own joke.

Nancy smiled and shook her head. "I have an idea. Come on!" She led her friends through the festival grounds, back over by the chili cook-off. "Mr. Wilson!" Nancy cried out as they approached their gym teacher.

Mr. Wilson was still standing on his tall stilts. He wasn't juggling small balls anymore. He still had the soccer ball going from hand to hand, but now he also had three butter knives spinning with it.

"Way to go, Mr. W!" George applauded as

the knives flipped through the air.

Without breaking his groove, Mr. Wilson waited until his right hand was free, then waved at George.

"Very tricky," Bess remarked as he caught a knife with that same hand an instant before it dropped away.

"Did you girls solve your mystery?" Mr. Wilson asked.

"Not yet," replied Nancy. "Remember how you said we could come ask you for help if we needed it?"

"Sure," the teacher said. "But what can I do for you from way up here?"

"We're looking for Natalie Coleman," Nancy told him. "Can you peer over the crowd and find her for us?"

Mr. Wilson scanned the festival grounds while still juggling with perfect timing. He looked left. Then right. Then turned around and looked left. And right. Finally he declared, "Natalie is with Suzie Park and Deirdre Shannon on the

Tilt-A-Whirl." He pointed with a knife, showing the Clue Crew exactly where they needed to go.

"Thanks a million," Bess told Mr. Wilson.

"You're welc—," Mr. Wilson said, suddenly stumbling slightly. He didn't fall off his stilts, but the soccer ball dropped out of his juggling, bouncing to the ground. In an instant, George swept the ball up and quickly tossed it back into his left hand, just as she had before.

"Now it's my turn to thank you," said Mr. Wilson with a smile.

"We're even," George told their teacher.

The girls hurried off to find Natalie at the Tilt-A-Whirl.

CHAPTER EIGHT

Torn Teddy

The girls caught up with Natalie, Deirdre, and Suzie just as they were getting off the Tipsy-Turvy Tilt-A-Whirl.

"That was an awesome ride," Suzie exclaimed, rubbing a hand through her windswept hair.

"I'm glad it wasn't any faster," Natalie said with a small shiver. "I was feeling a little green the whole time."

"I could have gone way faster," Suzie boasted. "I love spinning around." And, just to show how much she liked spinning, Suzie turned herself around three times quickly. When she stopped, she was dizzy and lost her balance. She fell into Nancy, knocking her backward.

With a lightning-fast move, George caught both Suzie and Nancy and set them both up straight.

"Oops, sorry," Suzie said with a shrug. "I guess I should leave the spinning to the rides." She laughed and asked Nancy and her friends, "Have you ridden the Tilt-A-Whirl yet? The tilt part was okay, but the whirling was the bomb."

"We haven't been on anything but the roller coaster," explained Bess. "We've been busy trying to solve a mystery."

"Oooh, what's the mystery?" Natalie was super curious.

"Well, you see . . . " Bess explained about Ned's missing tickets and then began to ask Natalie where she'd gotten so many of her own, when suddenly Natalie interrupted with a scream. A loud scream.

"Calm down, Natalie," Bess said. "I wasn't accusing you of taking the tickets." Then, under her breath, she added, "But you *are* our only suspect."

Natalie didn't seem to hear a word Bess said. She just kept screaming.

"What?" Suzie and Deirdre cried.

"What?" Nancy, Bess, and George cried in unison.

"My baby!" shrieked Natalie.

"Huh?" Nancy had no clue, literally, what Natalie was yelling about. Then she noticed that Natalie was holding a prize teddy bear from one of the carnival games.

Suzie and Deirdre escorted Natalie over to a bench and told her to sit down. Deirdre got Natalie a cup of water from the hot dog booth. Natalie took long, soothing sips and began to relax.

Once she'd calmed down, Natalie held out her stuffed bear. There was a hole in the back. Chunks of stuffing were spilling out of the bear's body. "I can't believe it! Who would do this to my baby?" Natalie took another drink of water. "Suzie won this bear for me at the Dart Dare."

"Natalie wanted a teddy bear so badly that she said she'd give me her new Goody-to-Go mini-bake oven if I would help her win one," Suzie explained. "She gave me a huge stack of tickets to use." Suzie sighed. "I thought I needed a lot. Some of those arcade games are nearly impossible to win."

"They aren't supposed to be easy," Bess agreed.

"I finally did it. You saw me!" Suzie gently touched her lucky necklace. "I won at the dart booth and then gave Natalie the bear." She grinned and looked at George. "I told you I want to be a caterer like your mom. I can't wait to try some experimental recipes in my new Goody-to-Go oven."

"Well," said George, leaning in toward Bess and Nancy so only they could hear, "that explains why Suzie had so many tickets. But we still don't know where Natalie got hers."

"It's possible that she took Ned's tickets and was using them herself," Bess suggested, rubbing her chin thoughtfully.

"I don't think so," Nancy said, her voice barely a whisper. Sitting down next to Natalie, Nancy asked in loud, clear tones, "Did you have this bear with you while you were on the ride?"

"No," Natalie admitted. "I set it down by the exit door. I picked it back up again after we'd finished."

"Did you notice the hole before you got on the Tilt-A-Whirl?"

Suzie jumped into the conversation. "I gave her the bear right before we got on the ride. There wasn't a hole. I'm sure of it."

Nancy simply nodded. "I need to think for a second." She walked a little way away from Natalie, Deirdre, and Suzie. Bess and George followed quietly, not wanting to interrupt Nancy while she was thinking.

Nancy pulled out her notebook and pencil, but before she could write down anything, Ned came running up to them.

"I was this close," he said, holding up two fingers an inch apart. "I almost knocked the milk jugs down, but one of them popped up at the last minute." Ned looked disappointed. "I bet I could win a bear if I tried just one more time." He looked directly at Nancy. "Any luck finding my tickets?"

Nancy didn't answer. She was busy writing

something down on the notebook page titled *Ned's Missing Festival Tickets*.

"Nancy looks busy." Ned pivoted to face Bess and George.

"She's thinking," explained Bess. "Sometimes Nancy spaces out when she does that."

Ned waved his hand in front of Nancy's face. She didn't even blink. "I wonder what she's thinking about," he remarked to Bess and George. "I hope it's about my tickets."

Ned left Nancy to her thoughts. "So? Did you find them yet?" he asked Bess and George. "Did Natalie help you solve the mystery of my missing tickets?"

"We never asked her where she got all those tickets," George admitted. "We were about to when she started screaming, and then Nancy asked her some questions and then—" George pointed to Nancy. "And then Nancy started thinking."

"Well," Ned replied, "we're wasting valuable festival time. Let's ask Natalie now! If she stole my tickets, I want them back." He looked over his shoulder to where Natalie was still sitting on the bench, surrounded by her friends.

Suddenly Nancy spoke up. The haze was gone from her eyes. She was clearly done thinking. "There's no reason to ask Natalie where she got so many tickets," she declared. "Natalie didn't take Ned's tickets."

ChaPTER NiNE

Mystery Madness

Nancy quickly drew a line through Natalie's name as their last suspect.

"If Natalie didn't take my tickets," Ned cried, raising his hands in dismay, "who did?"

Deirdre, Suzie, and Natalie looked over when they heard Ned raise his voice.

"What do you mean *if* I didn't take your tickets?" asked Natalie, clutching her bear, clearly mad. "I didn't steal anyone's tickets."

"You sure have a lot of tickets—," Bess began.

"And we saw you by the baseball booth right around the time Ned's tickets disappeared," added George.

"And we found a piece of Ned's ticket right

where you had been standing," Bess put in.

"And we eliminated Deirdre and Suzie as suspects." George took her turn. "Deirdre gets her tickets from her dad. Suzie gets her tickets from—you!" George pointed at Natalie.

"So where did *you* get *your* tickets from, Natalie?" Ned asked, putting his hands on his hips. "Are you sure you didn't pick up mine and add them to your collection?"

"Hang on a second!" Nancy stepped between

Ned and Natalie. She looked at Ned seriously. "We aren't accusing anyone."

Ned backed up a step. "I wasn't accusing her. I was just asking politely where she got all those tickets." He pointed at the large stack of tickets in Natalie's hand.

"I got them from Mr. Evans," Natalie declared.

"That name sounds familiar." Bess squinted as she tried to place the name.

"Isn't he the dad taking tickets at the Perfect Pitch baseball booth?" George asked.

"Yeah," admitted Natalie. "I really wanted to win a bear at the festival, but I knew my parents wouldn't buy me very many tickets. I needed to earn some money on my own."

Ned sighed. "I know how that is. My arms still hurt from all those leaves I raked for extra festival money."

Natalie sighed too. "My parents wouldn't give me any extra allowance, so I asked around school if there were any chores I could do to earn some cash. I found out that Mr. Evans would pay me to help paint the arcade booth counters." Natalie opened her hand, showing her tickets. "After school yesterday, I painted the red counter for the Perfect Pitch baseball booth and the blue top at the Dart Dare balloon pop.

"When we got to the festival tonight, I had the few tickets my parents gave me," Natalie went on. "Then Deirdre and Suzie went with me to find Mr. Evans at the baseball booth. He gave me the tickets I had earned." Natalie paused. "I handed a bunch to Suzie. And then Deirdre got some more tickets from her dad."

"So it was a coincidence that Natalie, Deirdre, and Suzie were at the booth at the same time Ned was playing," Bess said, considering Natalie's story.

"It also explains why they all had more tickets when we saw them after the roller coaster ride," added George.

"Since there aren't any more suspects, I suppose we'll never find out what happened to my tickets," Ned moaned. "I think I'll just go home now."

"Remember what I told you before?" Nancy asked him. "When we run out of suspects, we look for more clues." She held up her notebook for everyone to see. All the names were crossed off the suspects list, but Nancy had added two new items under the clues column: *String* and *Stuffing*.

"Come on." Nancy motioned to everyone to follow her. They went past the roller coaster, past the Tilt-A-Whirl, and stopped under the tree where Nancy had found the torn piece of Ned's ticket.

"What do you hear?" Nancy asked, tipping her head and cupping her ear.

"A bird with a really bad voice," said Ned with a laugh, and everyone agreed.

Nancy giggled as she pointed up at the big black crow, who was once again squawking along with the Best Buddies CD.

"Ned," Nancy said, looking high into the tree, "there is your thief."

ChaPTER TEN

Best Buddies

"What?" Ned said, clearly not understanding.

Natalie, Deirdre, and Suzie looked puzzled.

Nancy explained how she had solved the mystery. "I just knew Natalie hadn't stolen Ned's tickets when I saw the hole in her bear," she explained. "The missing stuffing reminded me that I had seen fluff in the crow's beak. I went over all our clues, and it was obvious that the bird must have taken Ned's tickets."

"The scratch in the red paint!" Bess declared.

"And the torn half of a ticket was found under this very tree!" added George.

"Exactly." Nancy pushed back a strand of her hair and placed her pencil behind her ear.

"Then I thought about the string my dad said he'd cut up. His string was missing too."

"I get it." Natalie jumped into the conversation. "You think that the bird took Ned's tickets off the Perfect Pitch countertop and left the scratch mark where her beak or claws hit the paint."

"Why would some bird need my tickets?" asked Ned, peering up at the crow in the tree. "And some string, and some bear stuffing, too?"

"I think I know." George asked Bess to give her a boost onto the lowest tree branch. She quickly shimmied up the tree. "It's building a nest!" George declared before coming back down.

Nancy smiled.

"Right!" Ned said. "That black crow was going around the fair collecting the things it needed to build itself a home." Ned put his arm around Nancy. "Thanks for figuring out the mystery, Clue Crew."

"We're glad to help," Nancy said. "I only wish we could get you more festival tickets."

"It's okay." Ned shrugged. "At first I felt bad about losing my tickets, but now I'm happy. That bird will have a new comfy nest thanks to my tickets. Its nest is way more important than me winning a prize bear." Ned looked at Nancy, Bess, and George. "You girls haven't played any games at the festival because you've been so busy solving my mystery. I'm going to go home." Ned couldn't stop smiling. "You should hurry up and play."

Bess checked her watch. "The festival closes in half an hour."

"We can split up our tickets and give you some, Ned," George suggested. "We're glad to share."

"We'll give you some too," Suzie and Natalie offered.

"You don't have to share your tickets," Deirdre told all the girls. "I have loads of them." She tore off twenty tickets and handed

them to Ned. "Come find me if you run out."
Ned thanked Deirdre and took the tickets.

"Go have fun," Deirdre said. Then she tore

off a bunch more tickets and laid them on the
ground under the tree. "These are for you, silly
bird," she called out. "You can use them for
your nest."

"I think the crow has plenty of tickets to build
with," George remarked. "Maybe we could leave
it some money for singing lessons instead."

Everyone laughed before rushing off to take advantage of the last few minutes of festival fun.

As they walked through the Fall Festival, Nancy linked arms with her two best friends. Bess was carrying the bear she'd won at the Perfect Pitch baseball booth, and George was carrying the bear she'd won at the Apple Attack apple bobbing.

"The festival is almost over and you didn't win a bear, Nancy," George remarked.

"That's okay," said Nancy. "I had a great time anyway. I love solving mysteries with the Clue Crew."

The girls decided that they would ride the roller coaster again to get a final view of the whole festival. As their car sat on top of the first big hill, they saw Deirdre finally win a bear at the apple bobbing. Suzie captured another one at the Dart Dare. And Natalie was at the Perfect Pitch baseball booth, holding three new, perfect bears in her arms.

Their car zipped around the track, and when it stopped, Nancy got out first. Just then, Ned came rushing up to her at the exit. "Nancy, I'm so glad I found you." He had his hands behind his back and was completely out of breath.

"Oh, no," George and Bess groaned.

"Do you have another mystery for the Clue Crew to solve?" asked Nancy.

"No," Ned replied. "Not this time. I came to give you this." He brought his hands out from behind his back. He was holding a big white stuffed teddy bear.

Ned held it out to her. "Thank you, Nancy Drew, for solving my mystery."

"Oh! You're welcome, Ned." Nancy took the bear from him, and Ned hurried away to ride the Tilt-A-Whirl before it closed.

"This was the best Fall Festival the school has ever had," George exclaimed.

"We worked hard. Now I think we all deserve a snack." Bess led the way to the cotton candy vendor.

Nancy hugged her new bear tight and said, "I think I'll call him Sherlock." She leaned in close and whispered into Sherlock's ear, "I can't wait for the Clue Crew's next mystery adventure."

A Carnival in Your Own Backyard!
You'll Have a Ball!

Even if you don't have a festival to go to, you can still have carnival fun at home. Creating a beanbag toss is both an exciting craft activity and a great game to play later with your friends. If you don't have any beanbags, you can use Ping-Pong balls or any other type of plastic ball. They'll bounce all over, so it'll be just as fun but twice as crazy!

You Will Need:

Beanbags or small plastic balls (Make sure you have extras!)

Large cardboard box (It should be at least the size of a microwave.)

Paint

Markers

Toss It Together

❀ First flip over the cardboard box so the bottom is facing up, and draw a small hole, a medium-size hole, and a large hole with a thick marker. The smallest hole should be a little larger than the bag or ball you're going to use, and the others should be much wider. Ask an adult to help you cut them out. Now label the different holes by the amount of points you want each of them to be worth—the smaller the hole, the more points.

❀ The rest is up to you. Decorate the box however you want with paint or markers. If you don't have any ideas, try making a clown face with one hole as the mouth and the other two for ears, or ask your friends what ideas they have. You can even paint the balls, too, if an adult says it's okay.

❀ As soon as the paint dries, you're ready

to play! Set up a line for the players to stand behind when they toss, and give them each two bags to throw before the next player in line goes. Once everyone has had their turn, tally up the score. You can play as many rounds as you like, or make the game harder by moving the players farther away from the box each round.

❀ If you're like George, you might even use math to win!